An Adventure With Pe[...]
At Hudson Ba[...]

KARLA LOCKE

PHOTOS BY JOAN SILLING

Published by Armchair ePublishing, Anacortes, WA 98221
www.armchair-epulishing.weebly.com

Graphics, Page Layout:
Tony Locke, Armchair ePublishing

Dedicated to Joan Silling
Photographer of Critters
World Traveler
Polar Bear Enthusiast
and Dear Friend

We would like thank *Polar Bear International* for providing the "Bear Facts"

www.polarbearsinternational.org

It was time for mama to take Peter and Penny to Hudson Bay for the winter. When the ice came, mama wanted to be close to their food.

Mama was hoping winter came early this year. Over the last few years there was less ice and she was starting to worry.

Peter and Penny were excited about their first trip to Hudson Bay.

It was fall, and the bushes were painted in reds and golds. Bears were lazing in the fall sun.

Bear Facts

Where do polar bears live?

Polar bears are found across the Arctic. They mostly live in areas with sea ice and ringed seals. There are five nations where polar bears live: U.S. (Alaska), Canada, Russia, Greenland (Kingdom of Denmark), and Norway (Svalbard).

Penny was looking forward to winter. It sounded like so much fun.

Mama said she would teach them to hunt at Hudson Bay.

And, they would have fun sliding on the ice.

Bear Facts

For at least 20 months, cubs drink their mother's milk and depend on her for survival. Her success at hunting is critical for her own needs and for teaching cubs to find food for themselves.

Mama told them to stay close as they crossed the river.

Hudson Bay is a large place and she didn't want them to get lost.

Bear Facts

Cubs generally stay with their mother for two-and-a-half to three years.

Bear Facts

In the water, polar bears rely on their fat layer to keep warm: wet fur is a poor insulator.

This is why mother bears are so reluctant to swim with young cubs in the spring — the cubs just don't have enough fat.

Penny stopped and balanced herself on a rock.

This new adventure was so exciting, and Penny wanted to look at everything.

Once they crossed the river, they stopped to snack on berries. Peter loved eating berries, they were so sweet and juicy.

Bear Facts

What do cubs eat?

While in the den, they drink their mother's rich milk, which is 33% fat! That's almost like drinking melted butter.

Later, after they leave the den, they will continue to nurse but will also learn to eat seals and seal fat.

What do polar bears eat?

Solid food comes when cubs are three or four months old and the mother makes her first kill of the spring.

Ringed seals—the primary food source of the polar bear—rest at breathing holes, cracks, or on the surface of the ice.

Bear Facts

Teeth. A polar bear's cheek teeth are sharp so they can shear off chunks of meat. Their canine teeth are long, sharp, and widely spaced so they can seize and hold prey.

After they ate, Peter and Penny played by the river.

The water felt cool and was fun to splash in.

Bear Facts

Head wagging from side to side often occurs when polar bears want to play. Adult bears initiate play—which is actually fighting practice or mock battling—by standing on their hind legs, chin lowered to their chests, and front paws hanging by their sides

Peter and Penny played their favorite game — Sparring.

Mama told them sparring taught them how to hunt and to protect themselves.

Bear Facts

Polar bear claws are thick, curved, sharp and strong. Each measures more than two inches (5.1 centimeters) long. Bears use their claws to catch and hold prey—and to provide traction on the ice.

Bear Facts

Polar bears' ears are small and round and their tails are short and compact. This helps bears conserve heat.

After such an exciting day, Penny was now tired and snuggled in the grass to sleep. Peter cuddled up next to mama.

As Penny fell asleep, she thought about what a fun day they had.

Bear Facts

Polar bear cubs make a variety of sounds from hums to groans to cries when communicating with their mother.

When they woke the next morning, mama told them she was going to show them one of the places she liked to play when she was a cub.

Bear Facts

Do polar bear fathers help raise cubs? No.

It was another day for a great adventure, Penny thought.

Bear Facts

Senses. A polar bear's sense of smell is very keen, and so is its eyesight and hearing. Heightened senses help bears survive in arctic conditions.

Penny stopped, she noticed some strange animals behind a fence.

"Mama, what are those strange animals over there," she asked.

"They are called humans," mama answered.

Curious Penny walked up to the fence to take a closer look.

Peter, who was more cautious, stayed behind Penny.

Bear Facts

In their first year of life, cubs are called COYs, which stands for cubs of the year.

"What is that human doing?" Penny asked, pointing at one of them lying on the ground.

"He is taking our photo," mama replied.

"Why?" Peter asked.

Bear Facts

Polar bears mothers usually give birth to twins.

Bear Facts

Polar bears look whitest when they are clean and in high angle sunlight, especially just after the molt period, which usually begins in spring and is complete by late summer.

Before molting, accumulated oils in their fur from the seals they eat can make them look yellow.

Polar bears have black skin under the fur, with a layer of fat below, that can measure up to 4.5 inches (11.5 centimeters) thick.

"Humans like to take photos and share them with their friends and family, to show them what we look like," mama explained.

"Why?" Peter asked again.

"They are curious about us," mama answered. "Some of them study us. They want to know how we live and interact with our surroundings."

"Why?" Penny asked this time.

"They want to learn more about us, like what we eat and how we raise our children," mama explained. "They are also studying our surroundings to see how we live in this environment."

Bear Facts

What do newborn cubs look like?

Like a big, white rat. Polar bear cubs weigh just over one pound at birth! They are about the size of a stick of butter.

They are blind, toothless, and covered with short, soft fur. They are completely dependent on their mother for warmth and food.

"Can we play with them?"
Penny asked.

"No," mama said.

"Why not?" Penny pouted.

"Someone would get hurt,"
mama replied.

Bear Facts

Nose-to-nose greetings are the way a bear asks another bear for something, such as food.

"They would hurt us?" Peter asked a little scared now.

"Not unless they have to," mama said. "We are big and strong, so they tend to be afraid of us."

Mama started walking away from the humans. "All right children let's go. There is more to see."

Penny took one last look before following her brother and mama.

Bear Facts

How big are polar bears?

Very big! Adult males normally weigh 350 to more than 600 kilograms (775 to more than 1,300 pounds).

Adult females are smaller, normally weighing 150 to 295 kilograms (330 to 650 pounds).

Peter was happy when he saw the old vehicles.

He couldn't wait to climb on them.

Penny followed, but wasn't as excited as Peter,
she just wanted to go watch the humans.

Bear Facts

*Where does the family go after they leave the den? They usually hang around
for a week or two while the cubs get used to the world outside the den.*

Mama kept a
close eye on
them while
they played.

Bear Facts

*The Russian term
for polar bear is
beliy medved, the
white bear.*

*In Norway and
Denmark, the polar
bear is isbjorn, the
ice bear.*

Mama called and said it's time to eat lunch.

Bear Facts

Polar bear silhouettes are distinct among bears. Their bodies are long and tapered—from their huge round posteriors to pointed, aquiline noses. Their necks are also very long, which is helpful when they swim and when they thrust their heads into holes to catch prey.

The next morning, Penny was excited to go watch the humans again.

Bear Facts

Mother polar bears lick their cubs to keep them clean. Cubs also lick themselves and each other, almost like cats do.

Outside the fence, they watched.

Bear Facts

Do cubs help with hunting? Not at first. They must learn to be quiet so their mother can catch a seal—And they learn how to hunt by watching her.

Penny found humans to be strange creatures. They walked on their hind legs, their fur was funny looking and were different colors. They didn't have paws, and were missing a tail.

Bear Facts

When swimming, forepaws act like large paddles and hind paws serve as rudders.

Peter and Penny decided to play for awhile, then went back to watching the humans.

Bear Facts

Polar bear paws are perfect for roaming the Arctic. Paws measure up to 12 inches across (31 centimeters) and help distribute weight when treading on thin ice.

When ice is very thin, polar bears extend their legs far apart and lower their bodies to distribute their weight even more. They are expert at placing each paw precisely and quietly when stalking seals.

Penny, now bored, sat by the fence and waited. What she was waiting for, she wasn't sure.

Finally a human walked up to the fence. Penny stood up to look at him. He was making an odd noise, it was as if he was trying to talk to her, but she didn't understand.

When he left, she felt disappointed.
She went to lie down next to Peter and mama.

Bear Facts

Polar bears' fur consists of a dense, insulating underfur topped by guard hairs of various lengths. It is not actually white—it just looks that way.

What strange animals humans are, Penny thought, as she drifted off to sleep.

Bear Facts

To the Inuit, the polar bear is Nanuq, *an animal worthy of great respect.*

After a good night sleep, mama took Peter and Penny to the bay.

Off in the distance Penny noticed the humans riding around on strange noisy cars instead of walking on their hind legs.

They would stop to
take more photos.

Mama sometimes felt
concerned about having so
many humans here.

She was afraid they would
hurt the place where they live.

Mama looked out over the vast bay. Each season there was less and less ice and she was getting worried.

She was concerned for her children's future, where would they live, where would they find food?

If it gets worse, would her children survive?

Bear Facts

During their time with mom, cubs learn how to hunt and survive in one of the earth's most challenging environments.

After a long day by the bay, mama took Peter and Penny back to sleep by the humans's camp.

Maybe the humans would get to know them better and help save the environment for her children, preserving their future.

Bear Facts

Scientists usually refer to how tall bears are by measuring them at the shoulder when on all fours.

Those heights are typically 3.5-5 feet for adult polar bears.

An adult male may reach over 10 feet when standing on its hind legs.

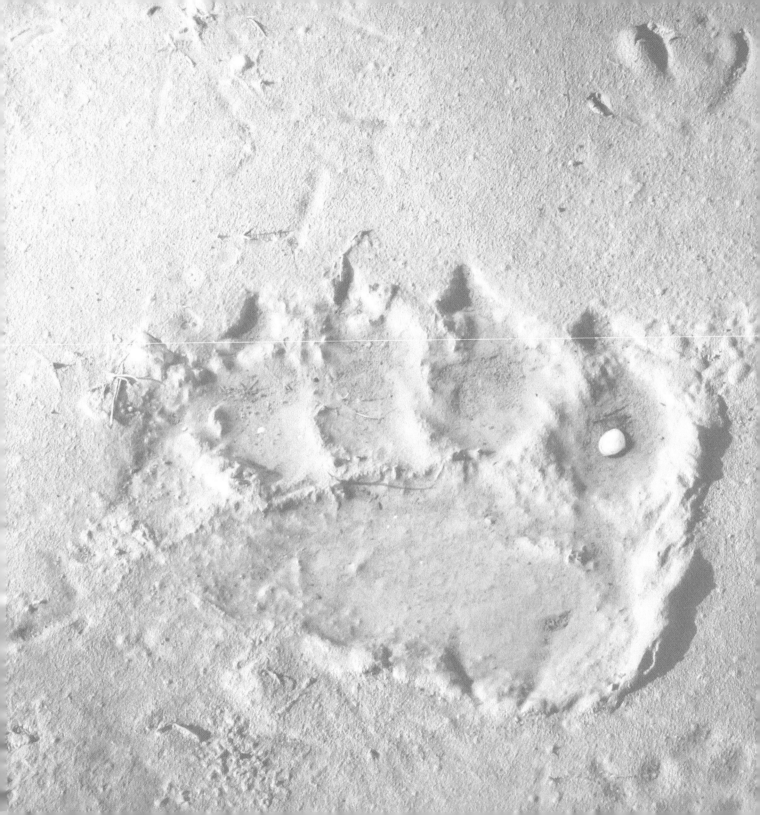

CPSIA information can be obtained
at www.ICGtesting.com
Printed in the USA
LVIC04n2134210915
455162LV00005B/10